The **Adventures**
of
Sammy and Vinney

The
Adventures
of
Sammy and Vinney

DIANE SICA

Illustrated by:
Kathy Kerber

authorHOUSE®

AuthorHouse™
1663 Liberty Drive
Bloomington, IN 47403
www.authorhouse.com
Phone: 1-800-839-8640

Published by AuthorHouse   03/19/2012

ISBN: 978-1-4685-6883-7 (sc)
ISBN: 978-1-4685-6880-6 (e)

CHAPTER 1

There once lived a little squirrel named Sammy. He lived in an old Oak tree with his mother, father, brothers, and sisters. Together there were seven of them. There were three boys, two girls, Mom and Dad. They were happy in their tree but as Sammy was the oldest, he was allowed to go out and roam through the forest. So one day he went out looking for an adventure.

He was walking through his part of the forest and met a raccoon named Vinney, who was about the same age as Sammy. They decided it would be a great idea to go on an adventure together. Two minds can think up more fun stuff to do than one, so they agreed on a direction and headed off. Before long they came to a quiet stream. Vinney, being a raccoon, knew he could swim very well since he had done it lots of times before.

Sammy, on the other hand, wasn't so sure about this water stuff. He knew it was good to drink but he had never been all the way in it, except to get a bath and then it was just little puddles of clean rainwater. They sat by the stream for a while and enjoyed the spring coolness coming off the water and all the smells of the new day. Without any warning, Vinney jumped in, KERSPLASH! Sammy was so surprised he almost fell in himself. He watched Vinney swimming around, having a good old time and wondered what it would be like to actually 'be' in the water up to his neck. The stream seemed to be moving very quickly and Sammy didn't know if it would be a good idea since he didn't know how to swim. Very carefully, he put his foot into the nice, cool water. He turned and watched Vinney, and decided it wouldn't be so terrible to get in the water himself but once he was in, he didn't know what he was supposed to do next. The water was deeper than it looked from on top and he started to sink a little bit as his fur got soaked through and his head went under the water. He pulled

himself out some, coughing and splashing and spluttering and needing help, but Vinney was busy swimming underwater and having fun and couldn't hear Sammy call for help. Just by luck, his foot brushed a big rock and he was near enough to grab onto a tree root sticking out next to it and he pulled himself out of the water. When he finally got back on dry land he shook himself off, three or four times, and promised to never do something that foolish again. Squirrels were not meant to go swimming! He sat on the bank of the stream where he was safe and waited for Vinney to finish swimming. When Vinney got out and shook himself off, they left the stream behind and began looking for another part of their adventure.

The pair walked along until they cleared the edge of the forest and came upon a beautiful green field of cut grass. They followed their ears to a babbling fountain sitting in a garden of lush flowers. Vinney was starting to get hungry and wanted to dig for bugs or chase butterflies but a smell caught their attention and made their tummies rumble. They lifted their noses and started to follow where the scent lead them to find out what it was. Out of the garden and down a path to a gathering place where there were benches for people to sit on and people all around, talking and reading and standing around this big shiny silver cart, which was where the wonderful smell was coming from.

Very carefully they crept up to the crowd around the shiny cart. Not too close though, they didn't want to get caught or stepped on. A nice little old lady turned from the crowd and

started walking to one of the benches. In her hands was a bag of whatever was in the shiny cart. She sat down and saw Sammy and Vinney watching her. She called to them softly and took something out of the bag and tossed it over to them. They jumped back! They didn't know what was being thrown at them. Their noses took control. They smelled the things the lady had tossed and it made their tummies do a rumble jumble! Sammy and Vinney rolled them around and played with them, but carefully because they were very warm.

When the things had cooled off some, the adventurers grabbed them and took big bites out of them. They were delicious! Sweet, salty and crunchy! Then it hit them, they had eaten these before, but never so warm and fresh! They were peanuts! Their parents had brought them home many times but they had never tasted this good. They gobbled up all they could stuff into their bellies and almost fell asleep where they sat they were so full. But, they managed to get back into the forest before it got dark and their parents started to worry about them.

Sammy and Vinney agreed to meet up again soon and find another adventure. Then they said goodnight and went home to their families. Sammy's Mom and Dad had started to worry a little bit, since it was starting to get dark, but he told them everything he had done and they were happy he had enjoyed himself, learned some new things and made a new friend. All in all, it was a great day for Sammy. He couldn't wait to do it again. After all, isn't that what kids like doing best, having adventures?

CHAPTER 2

It wasn't long before Sammy and Vinney met up again. They decided that since they had gotten so close to the city when they were in the park last time they would go a little farther. They met at daybreak and walked through the park and into a quiet street. They looked into boxes waiting to be picked up by the trash trucks. They looked in bushes and down alleyways between houses. They even went into a few alleyways, but didn't find anything fun to do so they kept going, looking for an adventure. As they were walking past two pretty little houses, they heard a noise down the alley between them. They went in to investigate, because that's what adventurers do. They got about half way down the alley and saw a big yellow striped tomcat jump out of one of the trashcans. They both froze on the spot! It was like their feet turned to cement! But the cats' hadn't and he was headed their way! All of a sudden, they found their feet still worked and they put them to use! They zoomed out of the alley looking for anywhere to hide from the monster cat! Vinney came upon a darkened window that was open and dove in. Sammy made it out to the street and straight up a huge Maple tree that was right next to a house that was so close to the house next to it he could easily make the jump and get as far away as possible from that nasty old cat!

Vinney, on the other hand, found himself in a strange, dark place that smelled funny. The window he dove into lead to the basement in one of the cute little houses he and Sammy had been walking past. It was cluttered with boxes, tools, newspapers, furniture, and lots of other stuff. Some of it looked very old and some looked like it was just put there. Vinneys' first thought was to get back out of the window, but when he looked back at the window he couldn't see a way to get back up to it.

Since he couldn't use the window to get out, Vinney decided to look around and check things out. "So this is what people stuff looks like", he thought to himself. None of it made any sense to him. There seemed to be an inch of dust on some of the things. If his mother ever came here, she would have a fit at how dirty it was down here! All of a sudden he heard a noise, like a creaking tree branch. He sat up very still and listened to where it was coming from. He saw a small beam of light moving around the room, but he also saw a larger patch of light that looked like it was high up in the sky.

Vinney searched in a panic for somewhere to hide. The only place that looked safe was a big old desk in the corner with a bunch of boxes on it, just by chance under another window. But, with no time to figure the maze of boxes on the desk Vinney just slid under the desk and into the farthest corner, where it was the darkest. Then he saw a pair of people feet coming down the steps. A people person must have come down because of all the noise Vinney had made when he landed in the basement. The people feet stopped at the bottom of the steps and a bright light shined into the corners of the room that Vinney could see. He made himself into the tightest ball he could and still be able to see what was happening.

The light came closer and closer until it was almost on him. He was very lucky to have a mostly dark coat with even darker stripes, but his mask would give him away in a flash! The

light came to the desk and stopped. Vinney thought he had it made and the people person would go away. He was wrong! He saw the people person get low to the ground where Vinney was, although he couldn't figure out how that worked. The next thing he knew the light was right in his eyes! He froze, trying to figure how to get away, when the people person put their hand under the desk! Vinney saw his chance and took action! He saw a crack of light from under the desk and ran for it! He scrambled to the top of the desk before the people person was able to get up straight and climbed quickly and carefully to the top of the boxes and out the window. He heard a huge CRASH from the darkness but wasted no time getting as far away as possible! The last thing the people person saw were Vinneys tail and a pile of boxes falling on them! And that was when he almost ran Sammy over.

Sammy had run up that big tree as fast as he could to escape the yellow

striped tomcat. Fortunately, the cat lost interest once he lost sight of Sammy. He was too old and fat to bother climbing up the tree when he had a nice bowl of cat chow and a soft pillow on a warm sofa to go home to.

On a good sturdy branch, well hidden from sight and in a nice tight clump of leaves, Sammy saw a birds nest. There were baby birds in the nest, chirping their heads off for something to eat. Sammy couldn't see the mother bird anywhere, so he sat next to the nest and chattered softly to the babies to quiet them and they stopped their chirping and listened to him. His father had taught him never to get so close to a nest of baby birds but he didn't want them to be so upset, so he risked it. The mother bird was not far away and when she saw Sammy so close to her babies she got very, very mad! She started pecking and screeching at Sammy!!

She flapped her wings as fast as she could, trying to get Sammy away

from her babies. Sammy backed up and tried to explain to the mother bird that he didn't want to hurt her babies and he had only been chattering to them to quiet them. Mama bird didn't want to hear any of it! She flew at him and pecked at him some more, and finally Sammy ran off to end the commotion.

Sammy climbed down to the bottom branch and looked around for that big yellow striped tomcat. He was nowhere to be found so Sammy scurried down the tree but before he got to the bottom, he ran into a not so friendly grown up squirrel. The grown up squirrel wouldn't let Sammy get down the tree. He chased Sammy back up into the tree. Sammy jumped from branch to branch, trying to get away from the mean old grown up, but the grown up was better at jumping through the leaves than Sammy and almost caught him a couple times.

Sammy found an opening and grabbed the chance to jump onto the rooftop just next to the tree and ran as fast as he could across the roof until he found a water pipe he could

use to climb down to the street. Sammy had decided it was time to find Vinney and get going towards home, but he was running so fast he could barely see where he was going and almost flattened Vinney! They were both so surprised they jumped back and fell to the ground, laughing 'til their eyes watered. When they could breathe again, they sat and talked about what each had done through the day. Although tired, they wanted to explore more, but the sun was starting to get low in the sky and that

meant they had to get back to the forest, and they didn't have a lot of time to get there.

They discovered a shortcut back to the forest and scurried as fast as their legs could take them to avoid being punished for being late. Sammy bumped into his sister not too far from home and she asked what he had been up to. Sammy said he would tell her at home so the whole family could hear at the same time. So his sister scurried home while Sammy and Vinney said their goodbyes for

the night and went back to their own trees and families.

Sammy sat on a branch outside his house and told his family what had happened to him and Vinney that day. His brothers and sisters oohhed and ahhed (they had never been so far from home because they were too young) and his Mom and Dad sat quietly and listened to how Sammy managed to get himself into trouble and out again all by himself, using his own smarts. They told him they were proud of him for using his wits and what he had learned growing up, but a little disappointed about his getting into those dangerous situations to begin with. Father forgot what it was like to be young and want to explore the world. Mother hadn't forgotten, but she didn't want Sammy to get hurt. They didn't punish him they just talked to him about all the dangerous things out in the world and to be more careful next time.

When Vinney got home he did the same as Sammy had done by telling about his adventure and his parents

weren't mad either. They just reminded him to be very careful when he was out in new places. Always look around and stay with his friend so they could keep each other safe so they could have more adventures.

THE END